The Boxcar Children® Mysteries

THE FIREHOUSE MYSTERY

created by
GERTRUDE CHANDLER WARNER

Illustrated by Charles Tang

ALBERT WHITMAN & Company
Morton Grove, Illinois

√5|4|00

Library of Congress Cataloging-in-Publication Data

Warner, Gertrude Chandler, 1890-1979
The firehouse mystery/
created by Gertrude Chandler Warner;
illustrated by Charles Tang.
p. cm. — (The Boxcar Children mysteries)
Summary: The Alden children draw upon their resourcefulness to save the
neighborhood firehouse from being torn down, while they also face a series
of mysterious incidents connected with it.
ISBN 0-8075-2447-6(hardcover)
ISBN 0-8075-2448-4(paperback)
[1. Resourcefulness--Fiction. 2. Fire departments--Fiction.
3. Orphans--Fiction. 4. Brothers and sisters--Fiction.
5. Mystery and detective stories.]
I. Tang, Charles, ill. II. Title.
III. Series: Warner, Gertrude Chandler, 1890-
Boxcar children mysteries.
PZ7.W244 Fi   1997   96-50218
[Fic]--dc21   CIP
                                                        AC

Cover art by David Cunningham.

6|9|04
√ 12|10|06

Contents

CHAPTER 1

A Trip to the Firehouse

"Look at what I found!" cried six-year-old Benny Alden, running into the old boxcar. It was a chilly Saturday afternoon, and his sisters and brother were sitting around a card table working on a jigsaw puzzle. They looked up and smiled at Benny, who was carrying a toy fire truck and wearing a firefighter's hat on his head.

"Hey, Benny," said twelve-year-old Jessie, "where'd you get that hat?"

"I was looking around in the attic, and I found it in an old trunk," Benny said. "You

wouldn't believe how heavy it is!" He pulled the leather hat off his head and handed it to her.

"Wow, it really is heavy, Benny," Jessie agreed. "I think it's a real firefighter's hat, not just a play hat."

As his sister turned the hat over in her hands, fourteen-year-old Henry spotted something. "What's that written on the inside?"

Jessie looked where he was pointing. "It says *James Henry Alden*!" she announced with surprise. That was their grandfather's name.

"Was Grandfather a firefighter?" ten-year-old Violet asked.

"I don't know. Let's go ask him," Henry suggested, walking quickly back to the house. The others followed close behind.

The children found James Alden sitting in his favorite chair in the living room, sipping a cup of coffee and reading the newspaper. They had lived with their grandfather since shortly after their parents died. At first, before the children had met him, they'd been afraid he was mean. So they'd run away and lived in an old boxcar they found in the woods. When Mr. Alden finally found them, they learned that he was kind and loving. He took them to live in his big, comfortable house. He even had their boxcar brought to the backyard so the children could play in it.

"Grandfather! Grandfather!" Benny cried, running ahead of the others and climbing onto Mr. Alden's lap. "Were you a firefighter?"

"Now, where did that question come from?" Grandfather asked, smiling.

"Benny found this in the attic," Jessie explained, holding up the hat.

"Well, would you look at that," Mr. Alden said, taking the hat from his granddaughter. "I haven't seen this in a long time."

"So it *is* yours! You *were* a firefighter!" Benny said with excitement.

"Yes, many years ago I was a volunteer firefighter," Grandfather said.

"What does that mean?" Violet wanted to know.

"I had my regular job during the day, running the mill. But at night and on weekends, I helped the full-time firefighters," Grandfather explained.

"Did you really fight fires?" asked Benny.

"A few," Grandfather said. "I did whatever they needed me to do."

"Wow," said Benny. The children looked at their grandfather with proud smiles. It was amazing all the things he'd done!

Grandfather placed the hat on Benny's head. "I have an idea. How would you like to go visit the firehouse where I worked? I'm sure Mike Reynolds — the fire chief — would give us a tour if he's not too busy."

"That sounds great!" said Henry.

"Hooray!" the other three shouted.

A few minutes later, the Aldens piled out of their car in front of the Greenfield Firehouse. It was an old red-brick building, covered with ivy. A garage on the side held the fire trucks. Inside, a man with silvery gray hair greeted them. He was wearing dark pants and a starched white shirt with a dark tie and a gold badge.

"Well, if it isn't James Alden!" the man said, taking Grandfather's outstretched hand and shaking it firmly.

"Good to see you, Mike," Grandfather replied, smiling broadly. "It's been a long time."

"Too long!" Mike said. Then he saw the four children standing behind Mr. Alden. "Are these your grandchildren?"

"Yes, they are," Grandfather said, turning to introduce them. "This is Henry, Jessie, Violet, and Benny."

"I've heard so much about the Alden family. It's nice to finally meet you!" said Mike.

Everyone smiled and shook hands with him.

Benny looked up at Mike, his eyes wide. "Are you a real fire chief, Mr. Reynolds?" he asked.

Mike smiled. "I am. And please, call me Mike."

"Neat!" said Benny. Then he frowned. "Why aren't you wearing a big hat and coat?"

"We only wear our gear when we're out fighting fires," Mike said. Just then a white dog with black spots came running up and put its paws up on Mike's leg. "Sparky!" Mike said, bending over to rub the dog's head.

"I knew there had to be a dalmatian here!" Jessie cried, leaning over to pat him. Sparky sniffed her hand eagerly and then licked it.

Mike turned to Grandfather. "So, James, what brings you by the old firehouse?"

"I was just telling the children about my days as a volunteer here," Grandfather said. "I thought that perhaps if you weren't too busy, you could give them a little tour and tell them what it's like to be a firefighter."

"I'd love to," said Mike. "How about if we go look at the fire trucks first?"

"All right!" cried Benny.

But as they were turning to go out to the garage, a man in a wheelchair came up and said, "Chief?" The man had reddish blond curly hair and a mustache, and was wearing the navy blue pants and T-shirt of a firefighter. With him was a gray-haired woman in a business suit. She had an angry frown on her face.

"Yes, Steve?" said Mike.

"This is Janet Lerner from the Greenfield town council. She needs to speak to you about something," Steve said.

Suddenly the smile disappeared from Mike's face. "Yes, Ms. Lerner, you called this morning. We'll talk in my office." Mike turned to Steve and the Aldens. All his cheerfulness was gone and his face looked gray. "I'm sorry, but this is something very . . ." he paused as if looking for the right word. "Serious," he said at last. "Steve, would you mind taking over for me?" Mike quickly introduced the Aldens.

"My pleasure," Steve said, as Mike led

Ms. Lerner into his office and shut the door.

Jessie whispered to Henry, "That was certainly mysterious."

Henry nodded. He, too, had noticed that Janet Lerner looked angry, and that Mike had seemed upset to see her. What was going on?

But before Henry could say anything, Benny called out, "Come on! Let's go see the fire trucks!"

CHAPTER 2

Just Like Real Firefighters

"Steve, are you a firefighter, too?" Violet asked as they followed him.

"Yes," he said, wheeling himself through a side door. "I used to be on active duty, until I was injured in an accident. Since then I haven't been able to walk. So now I work in the office, keeping the records, handling the schedules, taking care of the payroll — that sort of thing."

The side door led into the garage. "Look at that!" said Benny, staring up at the huge red truck in front of him.

"This is the ladder truck." Steve pointed to the long ladders on top. "We use it to get up to the tops of buildings to fight fires and help people who might be trapped inside."

"Is that the pumper?" Henry asked, pointing to a smaller truck.

"Yes," said Steve. "It's got a five-hundred-gallon tank of water in it."

"You use that to fight the fire, right?" Benny asked.

"That's right, Benny. Believe it or not, those five hundred gallons only last a few minutes," Steve explained. "We use that to 'knock down' the fire when we first arrive on the scene — to put out a small fire or try to get a bigger fire under control. But often we need more water."

"Is that what fire hydrants are for?" asked Jessie.

"Yes," Steve said. "When we first arrive at a fire, some of the firefighters go find a hydrant or another source of water. Using long hoses, the water from the hydrant is pumped through this pumper onto the fire.

The pumper provides the pressure to make the water go far and fast."

The Aldens noticed that the door of the pumper was open and a heavy firefighters' coat hung on it. On the floor below it was a pair of heavy boots already tucked into a pair of heavy pants. It looked as if someone had just stepped out of the clothes and left them there.

Violet was about to ask why when suddenly a loud bell filled the air, and then there was a voice speaking over a loudspeaker. "Smoke reported in the basement of the office building on the corner of Third and Elm."

Steve quickly guided Grandfather and the children off to the side of the garage. There they were out of the way, but could see what was happening. Several firefighters ran quickly in from the firehouse. In no time they had put on their heavy pants and coats. They grabbed their hats and oxygen masks and climbed onto the ladder truck.

One firefighter ran to the driver's side of the pumper and took off her sneakers. Now the Aldens realized why the clothes had been left on the floor that way. In one easy step, she stepped into her boots and then pulled up the pants. Next she took the jacket that was hanging on the open door and put it on. She jumped into the truck and put on her hat and oxygen mask, which were already inside on the seat. Another firefighter got in on the other side.

The ladder truck and the pumper pulled out of the garage, their sirens wailing.

"They were so fast!" cried Jessie.

"They have to be," Steve said. "Speed is very important when you're going to fight a fire."

"What were those masks for?" asked Benny.

"You mean this?" Steve asked, taking a strange-looking mask out of one of the lockers.

Benny nodded.

"This attaches to a tank of oxygen that's worn on your back," Steve explained.

"You know, Benny, smoke can be even more dangerous than fire," Grandfather explained. "It keeps you from getting the oxygen you need to breathe. That's why firefighters wear those masks."

Steve put a mask on to show the children.

"You look scary in that," said Violet. "Like a giant bug!"

"Or a creature from outer space," added Benny.

Steve removed the mask. "Sometimes at a fire, kids are afraid when they see us in all this gear. Then they run away when we're trying to help them."

"That's too bad," said Jessie.

Steve looked around at the children. "Would you all like to try on some real firefighters' gear?"

"Sure!" they said in unison.

Steve found four sets of jackets and pants and boots. With help from Grandfather, the children put them on.

"I can barely move, this stuff is so heavy," said Benny.

"It's made of special fireproof materials," Steve said. "Imagine wearing all that and running up stairs carrying heavy hoses!" He laughed.

Then Steve handed each of them a hat. "Do you know why the hats are shaped like that?"

The children shook their heads.

"It protects your head, and also allows the water from the hoses to run down the back, instead of into your eyes," Steve explained.

Wearing the gear, the children ran around the garage, pretending to fight a fire.

"I've got the fire hose," cried Benny, holding an imaginary length of hose.

"I'm going up to the top floor," called Violet, pretending to climb a ladder.

A few minutes later they saw the fire trucks returning. Everyone moved back against the side of the garage, out of the way.

Grandfather looked at his watch. "They weren't gone very long," he commented.

When the firefighter driving the pumper

had gotten out and replaced her gear, Steve
motioned to her to come over. "What happened, Christine?" he asked.

"Another false alarm," she responded.
Then she looked at the children, still
dressed in their big pants, coats, and hats.
"But if it had been a real fire, we would
have called you all to help!" She grinned.

"What's a false alarm?" asked Benny.

"It's when someone calls and says there's
a fire, but there really isn't one," Christine
explained. "It's dangerous, because chasing
after a false alarm might keep us from helping people who really need us."

"Who would call in and say there was a
fire if there wasn't?" asked Violet.

"It's a mystery to me," Steve answered,
his face grim. "I hope we find out before
they cause a real problem."

"We can help you find them," said Benny.
"We're good at solving mysteries!"

"In the meantime, how about getting up
into the fire engine?" suggested Christine.

The children's faces glowed with delight

as Christine helped them climb up into the front seat of the pumper.

"This is great!" said Jessie, holding the steering wheel and looking around.

"Yeah!" said Henry.

"I feel like I'm really going to a fire," Violet said.

Benny was so excited, he didn't even say a word.

"Sound the siren, Benny," Christine said, showing him the button to press. Everyone heard a loud wail.

"You look just like real firefighters sitting up there," said Grandfather.

"Come inside and we'll show you the rest of the station," Steve said.

The children climbed down from the truck and took off their gear. Then they followed Steve and Christine inside.

"This is our living room," Steve said as they passed through a room with large comfortable chairs grouped around a television. A firefighter was sitting watching a basketball game. In the back was a kitchen area with a large dining table, where a couple of firefighters were having lunch. "We're here around the clock, so when we're not out at a fire or taking care of the trucks, we cook our meals and watch TV just as you do at home," Steve explained.

"Looks like nothing's changed since I was here years ago," Grandfather said. The children noticed that he was probably right — it looked as if they hadn't even repainted the walls in a long time. Everything seemed run-down and shabby.

"What are those?" Henry asked, pointing at some tarnished silver cups on a dusty bookcase in the corner.

"Those are trophies the fire department has won over the years. Some of them are over a hundred fifty years old," Steve explained. Then he picked up a cone-shaped metal object. "Do you know what this is?"

The children shook their heads.

"It's a very old nozzle for a hose — probably a hundred years old. It's made of copper," said Steve. "And these are called speaking trumpets." He took a long silver horn from the shelf and dusted it off. "When we're fighting a fire, things can get pretty noisy. Nowadays when the chief needs to tell the firefighters what to do, we use hand radios. But a long time ago, fire chiefs used these." Steve demonstrated, talking through one end of the long silver horn. "Hello!" Steve's voice echoed loudly through the tube.

"Look at all the beautiful designs engraved on the silver," Violet said.

"Yes, these are real works of art," Steve said, replacing the speaking trumpet on the shelf.

"We've seen your living room and your kitchen, but where do you sleep?" Benny piped up.

"Upstairs," Christine said. "Come on up."

The Aldens followed her up a narrow staircase. It creaked as they walked. At the top were two tiny rooms lined with beds. They looked very crowded. "On the night shift the men sleep in this room and the women in the other," she explained. "And when the alarm rings, here's how we get downstairs in a flash." She led the Aldens to the end of the hallway, where a brass pole attached to the ceiling went down through the floor. A brass railing circled the pole. Christine lifted up the trapdoor around the pole, and the children peered down into the garage below.

"Want to slide down?" Christine asked.

The children nodded eagerly.

Christine showed them how to hold on to the pole with their hands and then wrap their legs around it. Then she, Jessie, and Violet slid down and waited at the bottom.

"I want to go next," said Benny. Henry helped him onto the pole. "Wheeee! This is fun!" Benny cried as he slid down.

Finally, it was Henry's turn. "Here I come!" he said.

"I'll take the stairs!" Grandfather called down.

The pole led the children directly back to the garage.

Benny was just about to ask if they could

climb up into the truck again when Mike Reynolds and Janet Lerner appeared.

"I'm sorry, but the only answer is to close this firehouse," Ms. Lerner said angrily. She turned and walked briskly out.

CHAPTER 3

Save the Firehouse!

The Aldens looked at each other in surprise when they heard what Ms. Lerner had said.

"What was that all about, Chief?" asked Christine.

Mike looked grim. "Ms. Lerner just told me that the town council is thinking of tearing down this building. They think it's too old and outdated."

"What do you mean, Mike?" asked Henry.

"Well, did you go upstairs?" Mike asked.

Henry nodded.

"Then you saw how crowded it is," Mike said. "A long time ago, not as many people lived in Greenfield, so there weren't as many firefighters. But since the town has grown, we need more, and we just don't have room to house them."

"Is that the only problem?" asked Jessie.

"There's also this old garage," Mike went on. "It was the right size back when they used a horse-drawn pumper."

"A horse-drawn pumper!" cried Benny.

"Yes," Mike explained. "Before gas-powered engines were invented, the pumps were pulled by horses."

"Prince and Duke," said Steve, who had just joined them. "The horses' names are painted on the wall over there. The pumper was on this side of the garage, and the horses were kept in a stable on that side. See the trapdoor in the ceiling?"

The Aldens looked up and nodded.

"The horses' hay was kept up there," Steve explained. "When the fire alarm rang, the firefighters backed the horses up to the pumpers. Then the harnesses were lowered from the ceiling. You can still see where the harnesses were kept up above."

"The problem now is that these garages aren't big enough for the huge modern fire trucks," Mike said. "We have to have trucks specially designed to fit, and that's expensive. The town council would rather tear this old garage down and build a new larger one."

"Why can't they keep this one and build another one somewhere else?" asked Henry.

"Well, we've thought of that, but it would cost too much — we'd have to buy a new piece of land," said Mike.

"But this building has so much history!" Jessie exclaimed. "They can't tear it down!"

"I'm afraid they will," said Mike. "And if it goes, I'm going with it."

"Mike!" said Grandfather. "After all your years on the force?"

"Maybe I'm getting too old, just like this building," Mike said sadly.

"There must be some way we can change their minds," said Henry.

"I don't think so," said Mike. "Ms. Lerner has already hired an architect to come up with plans for a new firehouse, and then the council will vote on it. She says this place is an eyesore, inside and out."

"An eyesore!" cried Violet. Then she looked around at the peeling paint and dusty lockers. "You know, I bet we could do something. At least we could fix the place up a little."

"Yeah. After all, we've fixed up an old library, an old motel, and even an old castle," said Benny.

Jessie, who loved to make plans, was already thinking. "A little cleaning and some fresh paint would make a big difference."

"I'm sure the firefighters would be glad to help," said Mike.

"I bet a lot of people in this neighborhood would be sad to see this historic building torn down," Henry pointed out. "We could pass around a petition to save the firehouse and get lots of people to sign it. That might change the town council's mind."

"We could even hold a Save the Firehouse Rally!" said Jessie excitedly.

"You know, it just might work," said Mike.

"That's my grandchildren," Mr. Alden said proudly.

The Aldens went with Mike into his office. In no time they had come up with several ideas to improve the way the firehouse looked. The rally was scheduled for the following weekend, out in front. The Aldens would make a big banner saying SAVE THE FIREHOUSE, and Mike would speak to the crowd. The children would work to fix up the firehouse as much as they could before the rally. The firefighters would help them.

As they left Mike's office, Henry turned around. "How long do we have until the town council votes?" he asked.

"Only two weeks," said Mike.

"Then we'd better get going!" said Jessie.

The next morning the children rode their bicycles to the firehouse, wearing their painting clothes. They had borrowed some of Grandfather's old shirts to wear as smocks. They were going to start painting the inside of the firehouse and garage.

"Hello," Mike greeted the Aldens, leading them to the garage, where several cans of white paint were lined up beside a couple of flat paint trays. "These were left from the last time the firehouse was painted," he explained. "Obviously, that was much too long ago."

Beside the paint cans were a bucket of paint rollers, a roll of masking tape, a ladder, and a stack of old newspapers. "Christine moved the trucks out so you can start in the garage. I'll send some firefighters down to help. Let me know if you need anything else," Mike said, going back into the firehouse.

"First we have to put down the newspapers," Henry said, "so we don't drip paint all over." The children covered the floor with newspapers and then put masking tape around the doorknobs and light switches so they wouldn't get paint on them. Then they started painting, rolling swaths of clean

white paint over the dirty gray-tinged walls. Benny and Violet did the lowest sections of the wall and Jessie took care of the middle. Henry climbed up on the ladder to reach the top.

"It looks better already," Jessie said, when the wall was halfway done.

"Trying to fix up this old place?" a voice behind her asked. "It's going to take a lot more than paint." Jessie turned around to see a short bald man carrying a small blue notebook with a gold symbol on the front. "Hi, I'm Ralph Frederick," he said, putting out his hand to shake hers. "I'm writing a book about the historic buildings in Greenfield and I've come to take a look at this one," he explained, a broad smile on his face. "Could you take me to the person in charge? Unless that's you," he added, a twinkle in his eye.

"No," Jessie said with a laugh. "I'm just helping out, along with my sister and brothers." Mr. Frederick smiled at each of the children. "I'll take you to see the fire chief. His name is Mike Reynolds," Jessie said.

She carefully put down her paint roller, then led the way inside. She stopped in front of Mike's office door. "Here's his office, Mr. Frederick."

"Thank you," he replied. "But please, call me Ralph."

"Okay, um, Ralph," Jessie said. "I'll buy a copy of your book when it comes out." She turned to go back to the garage.

"Thanks again," Ralph called after her.

By noon the Aldens had almost finished painting one side of the garage. Steve, who had been working in his office, came outside. "Aren't you kids getting hungry?" he asked.

"Yes," Henry said. "How about if we take a break for lunch?"

"I thought you'd never say that," said Benny, grabbing the big brown lunch bag they had brought with them.

"You can eat with me in the kitchen," Steve suggested.

Inside, Mike was sitting at the large kitchen table sipping a cup of coffee, and Sparky lay at his feet. "How's it going?"

Mike asked as the children washed their paint-speckled hands carefully in the sink.

"We're about halfway done," Henry said, taking a seat at the table beside Steve.

Jessie set the lunch bag up on the table and pulled out four cream cheese and jelly sandwiches, which she passed around. Then she pulled out a thermos of juice and a stack of plastic cups. Violet poured four cups of juice and handed them around.

"Mike, what happened with Mr. Frederick?" Jessie asked.

"Who?" Mike asked.

"That man who was writing the book about historic buildings," she said.

Mike's face looked blank. "I don't know who you're talking about," he said.

"I brought him to your office this morning," Jessie said. "He wanted to speak with you because he's writing a book about historic buildings."

"I never spoke to him," Mike said. "Never even saw him."

"Weren't you in your office?" Jessie asked, confused.

"Yes, all morning. But no one came by," said Mike.

"I don't understand," said Jessie. "I left him right outside your door."

"I wonder why he didn't go in," said Henry. "You know, something about him did seem a little strange."

"Is this a mystery?" Benny asked hopefully.

"No, Benny." Jessie gave Henry a look. "I thought Mr. Frederick seemed very nice and polite."

"You know," Mike said, "I was on the phone for a while. He probably knocked and I just didn't hear him."

"Yes, I'm sure that's it," Jessie agreed.

"Aw, nuts," said Benny. "I was hoping it was a mystery!"

"Well, Benny. There is one mystery. We still haven't figured out who's been calling in the false alarms," said Steve. "And there was another one last night!"

CHAPTER 4

Not Just a Bunch of Old Junk

As the children were finishing up their lunch, Sparky began barking. A moment later, the door opened and Ms. Lerner walked in. With her was a smaller, young woman who had short blond hair and a cheerful smile. She was carrying a large sketch pad and pencil.

"Hello, Mike," Ms. Lerner said. "This is Rebecca Wright, the architect I told you about yesterday. Do you have a minute to show her around?"

Mike sighed. He didn't seem happy to see Ms. Lerner again.

"I could show them around, if you're too busy," Henry suggested.

"That's very nice of you," Mike said. He introduced the Aldens to the two women. "Let me know if you need me."

While Jessie, Violet, and Benny went back to the garage to continue painting, Henry gave the two women the same tour he'd had the day before.

"See what awful condition this place is in, Rebecca?" Ms. Lerner said to the architect.

"Oh, yes," she agreed. Every now and then she would pause and make some quick notes on her pad.

"It really just needs some fresh paint and a little tidying up," Henry said. "Don't you think so, Ms. Wright?"

"You can call me Rebecca," she said, smiling. "That would help, I guess — "

"But we'd still need a new firehouse," insisted Ms. Lerner, frowning at Henry.

As they passed the shelves that held the

silver trophies, Ms. Lerner stopped abruptly. "Look at these," she said, carefully picking up a dusty silver trophy. She read the engraved inscription on the front. "This one is from 1865! These must be very valuable."

"Really? It just looks like a bunch of old junk." Rebecca picked up one of the old speaking trumpets and turned it over in her hands. She frowned a little and then stared at the speaking trumpet for a long time.

"I know a lot about antiques," Ms. Lerner said, studying the shelf of trophies. "Well, shall we go upstairs?"

Rebecca was still holding the speaking trumpet. "Oh, uh, yes," she said, startled out of her thoughts. She gently set the dusty trumpet back on the shelf.

When the tour was over, Henry went back to the garage. He was pleased at how clean and white the walls looked.

"We're almost done," Jessie called. She had taken Henry's place on top of the ladder while he was gone. "How was the tour?"

"It was okay, I guess," Henry said.

"What's wrong?" asked Violet.

"I just wonder if we'll be able to save this old place. Ms. Lerner seems determined to have it torn down," Henry said.

"That just means we'll have to work twice as hard," said Benny.

"Is there something else bothering you?" Violet asked her older brother.

"It's probably nothing," Henry began. "But when I showed them the silver trophies, Rebecca and Ms. Lerner just stood there and stared at them for a very long time."

"So? Those trophies are really neat," said Jessie. "They probably just wanted to look at them. I think you and Benny are both looking for a mystery where there isn't one. Like Mr. Frederick — you kept saying there was something strange about him, but I thought he was nice."

"Maybe you're right," Henry said, picking up a paint roller.

Soon, with the help of a few firefighters,

the Aldens had painted the whole garage. Everyone was worn out.

"It looks great!" Jessie said, sitting down to survey their work.

"Don't sit down yet," said Henry. "I noticed the sign by the door needs to be repainted."

The rest of the Aldens followed him around to the front, where they all helped to touch up the sign that read GREENFIELD FIRE DEPARTMENT. In no time it sparkled with fresh paint.

"I'm going to repaint those old window boxes," said Violet, heading over to the large windows on the side of the firehouse. The paint there was cracked and peeling. The boxes looked much better when Violet had finished with them, but still she wasn't satisfied. "I wish it weren't so cold out. These window boxes would be cheerier if they had flowers in them."

"How about if we get some evergreen boughs like the ones we had in the house during the holidays?" suggested Jessie. "We could put them in the window boxes. That would brighten things up out here. Remember how nice they made the town square look for the Winter Festival?"

"Yes! What a good idea," Henry agreed. "We'll get some tomorrow."

The children returned to the garage to clean up. Violet cleaned the rollers and Henry put the newspapers in the recycling bin. Jessie folded up the ladder. Then she helped put the cans of leftover paint beside the door that led into the firehouse. They'd continue painting inside the next day.

Steve came out to see how the children were doing. "The garage looks like new," he said.

Benny was just putting the lids on the leftover cans of paint when the fire alarm rang. Several firefighters ran out and started pulling on their gear.

"A kitchen fire on Chester Road," Christine told the children as she pulled on her coat.

"I wish we could go help," said Benny.

Steve smiled. "Maybe when you're older."

The children watched the firefighters getting into the trucks, which had been parked on the street while the garage was being painted.

"Why not now?" Benny asked.

"Fires are dangerous, Benny. It wouldn't be safe and we might be in the way," Jessie explained gently.

"Couldn't we just watch?" Benny said, refusing to give up.

Steve looked thoughtful for a moment. "You know, I think you could. I'll take you there in my car. We'll stay out of the way. Come on!"

The children ran to Steve's car, which was parked just behind the fire trucks. They were amazed at how quickly he was able to move himself from his wheelchair to the car, fold up the wheelchair, and put it in the backseat. The Aldens were ready to help, but Steve obviously didn't need it. The children climbed into the car just as the fire trucks were roaring off.

As Steve and the Aldens took off after them, Henry, who was sitting in the front seat, noticed something unusual about the car. "There are no pedals!" he said.

"Since I can't use my feet, I control the speed of the car and the brakes with my hands," Steve said.

"That's really neat," said Jessie from the backseat.

Chester Road was only a few blocks away from the firehouse. Steve stopped the car some distance from the fire trucks, which had pulled up in front of a small yellow house. On the lawn were a man, a woman, and a small child. The Aldens realized this must be the family that lived there.

"I don't see any smoke or fire," said Benny.

"That's good," Steve said. "It may already be under control."

Mike ran over and spoke briefly to the man and woman on the lawn. Then he directed a couple of the firefighters into the house.

"Shawn and Tom are going inside to check how bad the fire is," Steve told the children.

Meanwhile, Christine climbed up into the back of the pumper. "She'll control how much water goes through the hoses by using the knobs and dials up there," Steve explained.

A firefighter was hooking up two hoses to the pumper. Another firefighter attached the loose end of one of the hoses to a nearby hydrant.

A few minutes later Shawn and Tom emerged from the house and stopped to speak to Mike and the family. The man and woman looked relieved.

Then the firefighters went back to the trucks, and Mike began calling directions out to them. "The fire's out. There's just a lot of smoke inside. Christine, you and Stuart can go on back to the station. Shawn and Tom, get the fans."

"What are the fans for?" asked Violet.

"They're to blow the smoke out of the house," Steve answered.

The Aldens watched as Christine and Stuart disconnected the hoses and put them away inside the truck. Meanwhile, Shawn and Tom got a large fan out of the ladder truck and carried it inside.

"They didn't get to use all the hoses and everything," Benny said as Steve headed the car back to the firehouse.

"We never know how bad a fire is going to be, so we have to be prepared," said Steve. "Fortunately, today it wasn't too bad."

When the Aldens arrived back at the firehouse, they got their bicycles and got ready to go home.

"This has been a long day!" said Violet.

"Yeah, and I'm starving," added Benny. "Remember Mrs. McGregor said she was making chili for dinner tonight?"

"I'd hurry home, then, if I were you," said Steve with a laugh. "Chili is one of my favorite dinners, and I haven't had any in a long time."

"Really?" asked Jessie. "We're pretty good at making it, too — Mrs. McGregor showed us how. Maybe tomorrow we could make some for you and the other firefighters."

"I'm off duty tomorrow, but how about the next night?" suggested Steve. "If it isn't too much trouble."

"It would be our pleasure," said Henry.

And with that the children hurried home. They couldn't wait to tell Grandfather and Mrs. McGregor, Grandfather's housekeeper, about their exciting day.

The next morning the Aldens rode back to the firehouse, eager to get to work. When they got there, Mike was out in front with Sparky. Mike looked very unhappy.

"What's wrong?" Jessie asked.

"Come take a look," he said, leading the way into the garage.

As soon as the Aldens entered the garage, they saw what was bothering Mike. Beside the door to the firehouse, all over the floor, was a huge, messy puddle of white paint!

CHAPTER 5

"Just Give Up Now!"

"What happened?" Jessie cried. "We cleaned everything up so neatly before we went home yesterday."

"I know," Mike said. "I came in here after you left, and I was very impressed. Not only did the walls look much better, but you'd put everything away so nicely. Someone must have made this mess late last night, after I left. I'll go get some rags to clean it up."

As Mike walked off, Jessie turned to her

little brother. "You put the lids on the paint cans tightly, didn't you, Benny?"

"Uh — I think so," said Benny.

"Well, someone took them off again," said Henry grimly.

"Who would have done such a thing?" Violet wanted to know. "And why?"

"I don't know *who*, but I can think of a reason *why*," said Henry. "It must be someone who doesn't want us to fix this place up."

"Could the person who knocked over the paint cans be the same person who's been calling in the false alarms?" asked Jessie.

"Maybe," said Henry thoughtfully. "Both are bad for the station."

"Well, whoever it is, we're not going to let them stop us, are we?" asked Benny.

"No!" Jessie answered firmly. Then she saw Mike and Christine returning with a bucket of cleaning supplies. "Come on, let's all pitch in and clean this up."

It took Mike, Christine, and the Aldens quite a while to clean up the mess. When they were finished, they realized that there wasn't enough paint left to finish the project.

"I wonder if whoever made this mess wanted to make sure we couldn't keep painting," said Henry.

"I'll give you some money from the repairs fund to buy some more," Mike said.

"While we're in town, we can get paper and paints for our rally banner and posters," Jessie said.

"And evergreens to put in the window boxes," added Violet.

"That's a nice idea," said Mike.

"You know what else we can do while we're downtown?" Henry said. "We can start getting signatures on our petition."

"First we have to write it," said Jessie.

Mike lent the children a clipboard and some paper and a pen. Then he and Christine went back inside while the children talked about what the petition should say. Once they had decided, Violet carefully printed the three sentences at the top of the page in her neat handwriting:

We believe that the town council should not *tear down the Greenfield Firehouse! It is a beautiful historic building and an important part of our town.* Greenfield can find another answer!

Underneath, Violet drew several straight lines for people to write their names. The top four lines were filled immediately, as each Alden signed his or her own name:

Henry Alden
Jessie Alden
Violet Alden
Benny Alden

Next the children took their petition inside, and Mike, Steve, Christine, and all the other firefighters on duty signed their names.

"Look at all the names we have already," Benny said, holding up the page.

"Just wait until this afternoon," Violet pointed out. "We'll have even more."

* * *

When the Aldens arrived in downtown Greenfield, they parked their bicycles in front of the hardware store and went in to buy some more paint. The paint department was at the back of the store. On one wall was a rack holding small paper cards with different-colored stripes on them.

"What are these?" Benny wanted to know, pointing at the rack.

"Those are samples of different paint colors," Jessie explained. "For instance, if you want to paint something red, you take one of the red cards, and that shows all the different shades of red paint you can buy." She pulled out a card and pointed to one of the stripes. "See, there's a pinkish red called 'dusty rose.' " She pointed to another stripe. "And this really dark red is 'brick red.' "

"I bet I know what that bright red is called," Henry said, pointing to the center stripe. "Fire engine red!"

"You're right," Jessie said.

"Do they have all those colors here?"

Benny asked, looking at the cans of paint on the shelves.

"Not exactly," Henry explained. "When you bring the card up to the counter, they look in a big book — sort of like a cookbook — that gives the 'recipe' for that color. Then they mix certain basic colors together and give you your paint."

"Neat!" said Benny. "But what if you just need white?"

"They even have different shades of white paint," Violet pointed out, taking a card with stripes of white on it. "See, this yellowish white is called 'fresh cream,' and this pinkish white is called 'palest rose.' "

"But the kind of paint we were using was just plain white," Jessie said, "and there are cans of it right here." She picked up a can from the bottom shelf.

"Aw, they're not going to mix it for us?" asked Benny with disappointment.

"No, I'm afraid not," said Henry, taking another can from the shelf.

The Aldens decided that with the paint

that was left over, they would only need a couple of more cans.

Next they went to the art shop, which was just down the street.

"Hello, Mr. Sanders," said Violet to the man behind the counter. She liked to draw and paint, and came to the art store often to buy watercolor paints, drawing pencils, and large sketch pads.

"Hello, Violet. What can I do for you today?" the store owner asked.

"We need a large roll of brown paper to make a banner," she said. "We'd also like to get some smaller sheets of heavy paper to make posters."

"And paints — in lots of colors," added Benny.

"Yes, and some brushes," Jessie put in.

"The large rolls of paper are in the back," said Mr. Sanders. "Poster paper and paints and brushes are over there," he went on, pointing to some shelves behind the children.

"Thanks, Mr. Sanders," said Violet, as Jessie and Benny began to select some jars of brightly colored poster paints and some soft brushes. Violet pulled out several large sheets of paper, and Henry went to the back to get the large roll of paper for the banner.

When they were finished, the Aldens brought their selections up to the counter. Mr. Sanders rang up their purchases on the cash register, and Jessie gave him the money.

Their last stop was the nursery, which was a few blocks away.

As soon as they walked in, they saw what they were looking for. A large display had piles of evergreen boughs in different shapes and sizes.

"Look," said Henry, pointing to a sign. "They're half price, since the holidays are over."

"Great!" said Jessie.

The children selected two large boughs for each window box and took them up to the counter to pay for them.

"These will look nice with the red brick of the firehouse," Violet said.

By the time they'd gotten everything done, it was lunchtime.

"I'm hungry," said Henry.

"Wait a minute!" said Benny. "That's what I was going to say!"

Everyone laughed, because they all knew that Benny was always hungry.

"How about pizza?" said Violet, motioning to the pizza parlor that was across from the nursery. From where they stood, they could smell the delicious aroma of pizza baking.

"Let's go!" said Henry.

The pizza parlor was crowded, but Jessie found a table in the back and they all sat down.

"I want pepperoni," said Benny.

"Me, too," said Henry.

"Yuck," said Jessie. "I don't like pepperoni. I want mushrooms."

"Mushrooms!" said Henry. "That sounds awful."

"I know what we can do," said Violet, who hated to see anyone argue. "We'll get half pepperoni and half mushroom. And since I like my pizza plain, I'll just pick off the pieces of pepperoni and mushroom."

At last the steaming hot pizza pie arrived. The cheese was bubbling and gooey, and the sauce smelled spicy and delicious. The Aldens each picked up a slice of the kind they liked and started eating. Violet gave her extra mushrooms to Jessie and her extra pepperoni slices to Henry and Benny. In no time there was nothing left but a couple of crusts.

"That was great!" said Henry as he and Violet headed back to the firehouse to arrange the evergreens and start painting the banner and posters.

Meanwhile, Jessie and Benny went out to the corner to start getting signatures on their petition. It was a little bit chilly out, but they were wearing warm coats and hats.

"Save the firehouse!" Jessie called out.

"Come sign your name!" added Benny.

"What's that about the firehouse?" asked a man walking by. Jessie told him that the old building might be torn down.

"That's terrible," the man said. "I'd be

happy to sign." He took the clipboard and pen from Benny and read the petition. Then he signed and handed everything back to Benny.

"What's your petition for?" asked a woman behind him. When Jessie and Benny told her, she, too, signed eagerly.

The next person who came by did not want to sign their petition. It was Janet Lerner, from the town council.

"Still trying to save that old building? It's an outdated wreck," she said.

"We don't think so," said Jessie.

"And a lot of people agree with us," added Benny, holding up the petition.

Ms. Lerner looked angry. "I've worked long and hard to get a better firehouse, and I'm not going to stop now. You might as well just give up!"

With that she turned on her heel and walked down the block and into a small building. Jessie noticed that the sign on the door said REBECCA WRIGHT, ARCHITECT.

"That must be Rebecca's studio right there," said Jessie.

"Ms. Lerner seemed really angry," said Benny.

"Yes, she did," said Jessie. "I can't believe she told us to give up!"

"Do you think she knocked over the paint cans, hoping we would quit?" asked Benny.

"Maybe," Jessie said thoughtfully.

Almost everyone else who stopped to talk to the children happily signed the petition. Soon the page was almost full. "Look at all these names!" said Benny. He turned over the page, his eye running down the two long columns, each name in different handwriting.

"Let's go back to the firehouse and help Henry and Violet with the posters," said Jessie. "We can get more signatures tomorrow."

A few minutes later, Jessie and Benny were riding their bikes up the road toward the firehouse. The sight of dark green branches on the side of the building caught their eyes. "Look, Henry and Violet have fixed up the window boxes!" cried Benny.

They found Henry and Violet in the garage, surrounded by several colorfully painted posters. COME TO A RALLY! said one. HELP US SAVE THE FIREHOUSE! said another. Each poster gave the date of the rally and told people to assemble at noon in front of the firehouse.

"The window boxes look great," said Jessie. "And so do the posters."

"Look at all the signatures we've gotten," Benny said, holding up the page to show them.

"Good job!" said Henry.

"We were about to start on the banner," said Violet as she rolled out the long roll of paper in front of them. In pencil she wrote SAVE THE FIREHOUSE in large letters. Then all the children helped to paint the letters in bright colors.

It was nearly dinnertime when they were finally finished. They left the banner out to dry overnight. The posters were already dry, so they piled them in the baskets of their bicycles. On their way home, the children would hang them on trees and telephone poles throughout the neighborhood.

As the Aldens were just starting off, a familiar figure came walking up. "Mr. Frederick?" Jessie called out. "I mean, Ralph?"

"Hello, Jessie," he said.

"Mike told us he never saw you yesterday. What happened?" Henry asked.

"Oh, I decided not to bother him. He's such a busy man. But when I got home, I changed my mind. That's why I came back," Ralph explained. "After all, I have to get my book finished."

"Are you going to include the Old Town Hall in your book?" Violet asked.

"Uh — the town hall?" Ralph repeated.

"Yes, it's so beautiful with all the columns in front," Violet said.

"I never noticed," Ralph said.

"And the building next to it is at least a hundred years old," Henry added.

"Oh, really? I'll have to go take a look," Ralph said. "But I'm afraid I must be going now." And clutching his little blue notebook, he hurried into the firehouse.

"Hmmm . . ." Jessie said as they began riding home. "You know, I'm beginning to agree with you, Henry. Something about Ralph Frederick does seem odd. For someone who's writing a book about historic buildings in Greenfield, he doesn't know much about them."

"Didn't he seem in a big hurry to get away?" Violet added.

"Do you think he has something to do with the spilled paint or the false alarms?" Benny asked.

"Maybe," Henry said.

The children woke up bright and early the next morning. They were going to paint the living room of the firehouse that day and knew they had a lot of work ahead of them. Jessie tucked the petition carefully in her knapsack, so they would be able to get more signatures.

But as they rode up to the front of the firehouse an awful surprise awaited them.

"What happened to the window boxes?" cried Violet, who was the first to notice.

The beautiful evergreens had been knocked to the ground, where they lay bent and trampled, covered with dirt.

CHAPTER 6

"*A Whole Lot of Money!*"

"Not again!" said Jessie. "Yesterday the paint was all a mess, and today it's the window boxes!"

"What do you think happened?" asked Violet.

The children knelt down and examined the trampled evergreens. "Look at the ground under the windows. It's all scuffed up with footprints," said Henry.

"Everything we do to improve the firehouse backfires," said Violet with a sigh.

"Maybe that's the person's plan," said Henry.

"Well, we're not going to give up," said Jessie. "That's just what someone wants us to do."

"That's what Janet Lerner said yesterday!" Benny exclaimed. "She said, 'You might as well just give up!' "

"I wonder what she was doing downtown," said Violet.

"She was going to Rebecca Wright's studio. You know, the architect. It's near where we were standing," said Jessie.

"You know, we have to go downtown again today to buy the ingredients for the chili we promised Steve. Maybe while we're there we should talk to Rebecca," suggested Henry. "She might be able to change Ms. Lerner's mind."

"I doubt it," said Jessie. "Ms. Lerner seemed pretty angry yesterday."

"It's worth a try," said Violet. "We can also pick up some more evergreens. It's a good thing they were half-price!"

They rode their bikes downtown, and Jessie showed the others where Rebecca's studio was. The Aldens entered the building and found themselves in a large, airy room, with a slanted drafting table in the center and some other tables along the walls. Large drawings of buildings were spread out on the tables or rolled up in stacks. At the back they could see a smaller office.

"Rebecca must be back there," said Jessie. "It sounds like she's talking on the telephone."

As the children waited for her to finish her phone call, they couldn't help hearing what she was saying.

"I know, isn't it great?" she said, excitement in her voice. "We'll finally have some money. A whole lot of money, if everything goes as planned."

Benny was looking at a can of colored pencils, and just then he knocked them over.

"It sounds as if someone's come in," they

heard Rebecca say. "I'll call you later." In a moment she came out from a door at the back.

"Hello," she said. "You're the kids from the firehouse, aren't you? The Aldens?"

"Yes. We want to talk to you about the firehouse," said Henry.

"Isn't it exciting?" said Rebecca. "A brand-new building!"

"But lots of people like the old building," said Jessie. "Just look." She pulled the petition out of her knapsack and put it on Rebecca's drafting table.

"Yes, I see," said Rebecca, looking at the page. "But why are you telling me this?"

"We were hoping you could change Ms. Lerner's mind about tearing the firehouse down," Henry said.

Rebecca shook her head. "You don't understand. I'm just starting out as an architect. This is a really big break for me." She picked up her sketch pad and put it on her drafting table. "Look at my sketches for the new firehouse. It's going to be wonderful."

The children crowded around as Rebecca

flipped one page after another. "Here's the new entry hall," she said. "And here's the kitchen area." Her drawings were beautiful, and the children could see there was much more space and plenty of windows. But still, her plans meant that the old firehouse would be destroyed.

"Wait a minute. Aren't those the trophies?" asked Benny, pointing to one of the drawings. It showed several of the trophies, drawn in great detail.

"Yes," said Rebecca as the children looked more closely. "I'm going to design a special case for those."

"This drawing has much more detail than the others. It must have taken you a long time," said Violet.

"You told Ms. Lerner that you thought the trophies were just a bunch of old junk," Henry said, recalling what Rebecca had said while he was showing her around the firehouse.

"I've just begun to learn that old things can be valuable," said Rebecca. "And beautiful," she added. Quickly she tucked the drawing of the trophies under the rest of the plans. "Listen, if that's all you came for, you might as well go. As I said, this is my first big break. I'll do anything to hang on to this project. *Anything*." She looked very serious.

"All right," said Jessie. "I'm sorry we couldn't change your mind."

"And I'm sorry I couldn't change yours," Rebecca said.

The Aldens went from Rebecca's studio to the nursery to pick up more evergreens. The woman behind the counter was surprised to see them again. "Weren't you just in here buying some of these yesterday?" she asked.

"Yes," said Henry. "But there was a little . . . um, problem. We need more."

The grocery store was right next to the nursery. The Aldens went inside, and Jessie picked up a basket.

"We'll need some ground beef," said Henry.

"While you're getting that, I'll get some canned tomatoes, beans, and some spices," said Jessie.

"I'll pick out an onion and a green pepper," Violet said.

"What can I do?" asked Benny.

"Why don't you go get a box of rice and some cheddar cheese to serve with the chili," Henry suggested.

In no time, the children had collected everything they needed for the chili and were back on their bicycles, heading back to the firehouse. As they rode, they talked about their visit to Rebecca's studio.

"Remember what she was saying on the phone when we came in?" asked Henry. "Something about money."

"Yes. I wonder what she was talking about," Jessie said.

"I've been thinking about the drawing of the trophies," said Violet. "It was so carefully done, and yet she didn't seem to want to talk about it."

"I noticed that, too," Jessie agreed. "And she made some comment about old things being valuable. . . . I had the feeling that she meant more than she was saying."

Soon the children arrived at the firehouse. Christine and Shawn were there, putting on their gear. They weren't moving as quickly as usual.

"Is there a fire?" asked Benny.

"No," said Christine with a smile. "Today's job is a little unusual. If you want to come watch, we'll be on Oak Lane." A moment later, she and Shawn drove off in the truck.

"That sounds mysterious!" said Violet. "What do you think they're doing?"

"Only one way to find out," said Henry. And so after quickly putting away their groceries, the Aldens got back on their bicycles. Oak Lane wasn't too far away. A few minutes later they were coasting down the road, parking their bikes near the fire truck.

Shawn was getting some tools out of the back of the truck. Christine was standing in the road, next to a sewer. She was talking to an attractive woman with brown curly hair. Christine motioned to the children to join her. "This is Mrs. Berg. She'll tell you what's going on."

Mrs. Berg took up the story. "This morning I heard some little noises down in the sewer. At first I thought I was imagining things. But when I went closer and peered down inside, I realized what it was. A kitten has fallen into the sewer."

"Oh, no!" said Jessie. "How sad."

"Luckily, there's a dry ledge on the side of the sewer, so he'll be okay for a while," said Mrs. Berg.

"Don't worry," said Christine. "We'll get the little guy out."

Shawn had taken the tools over to the sewer and was prying the grating off. As Mrs. Berg and the Aldens watched, he and Christine slowly lifted the heavy piece of metal. Then Christine reached in and pulled out the tiny kitten.

"How sweet," Violet said, as Christine held up the kitten for Mrs. Berg and the children to see.

"He doesn't seem to be hurt," said Christine. "We'll call the animal shelter to see if anyone has lost a kitten."

"I've heard of firefighters rescuing cats stuck up in trees, but not in sewers!" said Benny, surprised.

"People call us whenever they need something done and don't know who else to call," said Shawn.

The Aldens rode their bikes back to the firehouse and arranged the new evergreens in the window boxes. "I hope nothing happens to these," said Violet. Then they joined Steve for lunch. The Aldens all sat around the kitchen table, eating the tuna fish sandwiches Mrs. McGregor had made for them.

When they were finished with lunch, the children started making the chili, since it would need several hours to simmer before dinnertime. With Steve supervising, Henry carefully turned on the stove. Then he put the ground beef in a large pot and put it on the stove. Soon it began to sizzle, and Henry stirred it with a long wooden spoon.

Meanwhile, Jessie got out a cutting board. She chopped up the onion and green pepper, being extra careful with the knife. When she was done, she slid the vegetable pieces off the cutting board and into the pot with the browned meat. Soon a wonderful smell filled the room.

When the onions and peppers were cooked, Violet opened the cans of tomatoes and beans and dumped them into the pot. Then Benny carefully measured out the spices — cumin, garlic, and chili powder — with measuring spoons. Standing up on a chair so that he could reach, he dropped each spoonful into the pot and stirred it with the wooden spoon.

Jessie turned down the heat under the pot. "Now that just needs to simmer for a few hours, and it will be ready for dinner."

"It smells delicious," said Steve. "I can't wait!"

While the chili simmered, the Aldens began to paint the inside of the firehouse. Some of the firefighters had prepared the rooms while the Aldens were away. They had moved the furniture away from the walls and draped it with big white sheets. They had also covered the floor with newspapers and put tape around all the doorknobs, windows, and light switches.

The Aldens spent the rest of the afternoon painting. With the help of the firefighters, the downstairs was almost completed by dinnertime.

"We'll finish up here tomorrow morning and then move on to the upstairs," said Jessie as they packed up their things. "We'll finish just in time for the rally Saturday!"

"Now it's time to finish preparing dinner," said Henry.

The Aldens washed their hands carefully in the kitchen. Then Henry put a large pot of water on the stove to boil, before pouring in some rice. Benny grated the sharp cheddar cheese and put it in a bowl. Meanwhile, Jessie and Violet were setting the table. Besides Steve, there were six firefighters who would be joining them for dinner.

"It's a good thing we made a big pot of

chili," said Violet as she and Jessie laid plates around the kitchen table. Beside each plate they put a knife, fork, and spoon, and a paper napkin. Then they filled glasses with water or milk and put them around the table, too.

"The rice is ready," said Henry finally.

Jessie peered into the chili pot and stirred the mixture with the wooden spoon. "The chili looks just right," she said.

"Dinnertime!" Benny called out.

Steve came out of his office. "Smelling that wonderful smell all afternoon has been making me hungry," he said as he wheeled up to the table.

One by one, the other firefighters came and sat down. A couple of them had been watching TV in the living room, and one had been reading a book upstairs. The others had been working on one of the trucks in the garage.

Henry served rice into each bowl and handed it to Jessie. She spooned the steaming hot chili over the rice. Then Benny sprinkled the top of each bowl with grated cheese. Violet carried the bowls to the table and handed one to each firefighter.

Soon all the bowls had been filled and the Aldens sat down at the table with the others.

"Mmmm!" said Tom, tasting his first spoonful. "This is delicious!"

"Sure is," Shawn agreed. "Even better than the chili I make."

Jessie took a taste. "Not bad," she admitted, turning to her sister and brothers. "But Mrs. McGregor still makes it the best."

Several of the firefighters had seconds, and Steve even had a third bowl.

When everyone had eaten his or her fill of the delicious chili, the Aldens cleared the dishes away. Then Steve got a large container of mint chip ice cream out of the freezer and served everyone a large scoop.

"This is the perfect way to finish off the meal!" said Violet, putting a spoonful of the green speckled ice cream in her mouth.

At last even Benny was full. Jessie and

Henry washed the dishes, while Benny and Violet and a couple of the firefighters dried them and put them away.

When the kitchen was neat and clean, Benny tried to stifle a yawn, but Jessie spotted it. "I think it's time we went home. It's been a busy day."

"Thank you so much for making dinner," Tom said, and the other firefighters chimed in with their thanks, too.

"Yes," said Steve. "You kids are great cooks!"

The next morning, the Aldens were happy to see the evergreens still decorating the window boxes.

"The place looks great, so far," Mike told them as they started painting. "Keep up the good work."

"Thanks," said Henry.

A couple of firefighters helped finish painting the downstairs. As they were all taking a break for lunch, one of the men turned to Jessie. "Hey, I hear you kids have a petition to save the firehouse. I'd like to sign."

"Great, I'll get it," said Jessie, running to fetch her knapsack from the garage. But when she opened it and looked inside, the petition was gone!

CHAPTER 7

Lost — and Found!

"It's got to be here some-where," Jessie muttered to herself. She took everything out of her knapsack. But the petition wasn't there. "How can this be?" she said to herself. "I never lose things."

Jessie searched everywhere in the garage. Maybe the petition had fallen out somehow. But it was nowhere to be found.

Jessie ran back into the firehouse to tell the others.

"What do you mean the petition's missing?" asked Henry. "Didn't you have it in your knapsack?"

"Yes," said Jessie. "But now I can't find it."

The Aldens could see how upset their sister was. "Let's go out to the garage and take another look," said Violet. "Maybe you just misplaced it somehow."

But, back in the garage, the others had no better luck than Jessie.

"Where was the knapsack?" Henry asked.

"Right here," said Jessie, pointing to the floor at her feet.

Henry looked at the wide-open garage doors. "So your knapsack was sitting out in the garage all morning while we were inside painting?"

"Yes," Jessie said.

"I hate to say this," Henry began. "But . . . I wonder if someone took the petition."

"You think someone stole it?" asked Benny.

"I can't think of any other explanation," Henry said as they went back inside the firehouse.

"But who do you think would have taken it?" asked Jessie.

"I don't know," said Henry. "But probably the same person who's been doing the other things to harm the firehouse. Without that petition, the town council won't know how many people want to save this place."

"Well, there's just one thing to do," said Jessie. "Tomorrow I'll go out and get all those signatures again. The petition was my responsibility, and so it's my fault it's gone."

"We'll all help get signatures," said Henry. "Whoever's trying to stop us from saving the firehouse doesn't know one important thing about the Aldens."

"What's that?" asked Violet.

"We don't give up!" said Henry.

Just then they heard Sparky barking and the door opened. It was Rebecca Wright, carrying her sketch pad and a big bag.

After greeting the Aldens, she turned to Steve, who had come to help them paint.

"Mind if I take another look around?" she asked.

"Of course not," Steve replied. "You can leave your things here on the couch if you'd like."

The Aldens watched as Rebecca put down her bag. Then, sketch pad in hand, she began to walk around. She paused in front of the antique silver pieces for several minutes, a thoughtful look on her face.

"Is anything wrong?" Henry asked, seeing how closely she was studying them.

Rebecca didn't answer.

"Rebecca?" Jessie said.

She jumped. "What — oh, I'm sorry, I was just thinking. Did you ask me something?"

"I just wondered if anything was wrong," Henry said.

Rebecca didn't answer for a moment. She looked again at the silver pieces. "No, no, I guess not," she said at last.

Rebecca headed upstairs just as the

Aldens had finished packing up the supplies to bring up there.

"I don't know about you guys, but I'm tired of painting," said Benny, putting down his brush and sitting down on the couch. "I wanted to learn about firefighting, not painting."

"I wouldn't mind taking a break myself," said Violet.

"That's fine," said Jessie. "Henry and I will take the supplies upstairs and start getting ready to paint."

Steve rolled up beside Benny and Violet. "Well, if you're going to be firefighters, then you need to know the five most important safety rules," he said. "What do you think the most important rule is?"

"Never play with matches?" asked Violet.

"That's right. Lots of fires start that way," Steve told them. "Stay away from open flames, like barbecue grills. Last night, when you were making the chili, I was glad that you asked me for help before you turned on the stove. You should never use the stove without an adult's help."

"We always ask Grandfather or Mrs. McGregor or Aunt Jane to help us," said Violet.

"Now for the next rule. What should you do if you think there's a fire in the house?" asked Steve.

"Call the fire department?" asked Benny.

"Even before that," said Steve.

"Get out?" Violet asked.

"Yes," Steve said. "Get out quickly. If it's smoky, crawl low on the ground. Don't go back in even if you've forgotten something. Wait until an adult tells you it's safe."

"Why do you crawl?" Benny wanted to know.

"Because it's very dangerous to breathe smoke," Steve explained. "Since smoke rises, the clearest air is near the ground."

"I get it," said Benny.

Steve went on, "Make sure you know at least two ways out. You should even have some practice fire drills with your family."

"Then do you call the fire department?" asked Benny.

"Yes, that's the next rule. As soon as

you're safe, call the fire department right away," said Steve. "In many towns you can just dial 9-1-1 for any kind of emergency. Make sure the emergency numbers are taped to the phone."

"What about 'stop, drop, and roll'?" asked Violet.

"What's that?" asked Benny. "Sounds like a new dance!"

Steve laughed. "That's rule number four, and it's what you do if your clothes catch on fire. You should never run, because that will only make the fire burn more. Violet, why don't you show Benny?" Violet stood up.

"First you stop," said Steve. Violet stood very still.

"Then you drop," he said. Violet dropped to the floor and lay down.

"Then you roll," he finished, as Violet rolled on the floor. "Rolling on the ground will put out the flames. Be sure to cover your face with your hands."

"Now I get it," said Benny, as he rolled on the floor next to Violet.

"And the last rule is, make sure your Grandfather changes the batteries in your smoke alarms every year," said Steve. "Now, can you kids repeat those rules back to me?"

One by one, Violet and Benny recited each rule.

"You're good students. Now how about a cup of hot cocoa?" Steve asked.

"That sounds great," said Benny, going with Steve into the kitchen. "I'll get one for you, Violet."

A few minutes later, Benny returned with two steaming mugs of cocoa.

"Benny," Violet whispered, her voice tense. "Come here, quick."

Benny looked at his sister. She was sitting on the couch staring at Rebecca Wright's bag. "What is it?" Benny asked, hurrying over to her. "Why are you acting so strange?"

"Look what's sticking out of Rebecca's bag," said Violet.

"What do you mean?" Benny asked.

"Just look," said Violet. "Quick, before she comes back downstairs."

Benny looked, and his eyes grew big and round. He saw immediately why his sister was behaving so oddly. Sticking up out of Rebecca's bag was a folded piece of paper. On the paper he could see Violet's handwriting at the top and a long column of signatures underneath. It was the petition! "What's that doing in there?" he asked.

"Shhhh! She'll hear you," Violet said, her voice hushed.

"What's that doing in there?" Benny repeated in a whisper.

"That's just what I was wondering," Violet whispered back.

"Rebecca must have taken it," said Benny. "But why?"

"That doesn't matter right now," said Violet. "What matters is, how are we going to get it back?"

"I think we should just ask her for it," said Benny. "After all, it's ours, isn't it?"

"Yes, but — " Violet started to say. But it was too late. Rebecca had come down the stairs, and she was heading right for them.

CHAPTER 8

A Broken Lock

"See you all later," Rebecca said, picking up her bag and slinging it over her shoulder.

Benny looked at Violet. Rebecca was about to leave, and she still had their petition!

Before Violet could stop him, Benny blurted out, "Rebecca, isn't that our petition in your bag?"

Rebecca turned around, her face pink. "Oh, my goodness, that's right." She laughed uncomfortably. "I feel so silly! I

forgot I had brought it to give back to you."
She put down her bag, pulled out the petition, and handed it to Benny.

"Why do you have it?" asked Benny.

"Why? Well, I just found it — " Rebecca started to say, when Jessie came down the stairs and interrupted her.

"Is that our petition?" Jessie said. "Oh, I'm so glad it's not gone!" She smiled gratefully at Rebecca. "That would be a lot of signatures to get all over again."

"Yes, I'm glad you have it back," said Rebecca. But she didn't look happy at all. "I've got to run." A moment later she was gone.

"Can you believe Rebecca had our petition?" said Violet.

"Do you believe that she really just 'found it' like she said?" asked Benny.

"Why would she lie?" asked Jessie. "Anyway, she gave it back to us."

"But she wasn't going to," Benny said. "She wouldn't have if Violet hadn't seen it in her bag."

"And you hadn't asked her for it," added Violet.

"You think she meant to keep it?" asked Jessie.

"I don't know, but when Benny asked her about it, she had a funny expression on her face. I think she looked kind of . . . guilty," Violet said.

When Henry came downstairs, they told him all about what had happened. "Do you think Rebecca could be the one who's done all the harmful things to the firehouse?" he asked.

"Maybe," said Jessie. "After all, she has a good reason. If we fix this place up, and convince the town council not to build a new building, then she's lost a big project."

"Remember she said this would be a big break for her," said Henry.

"She also said she'd do anything to hold on to it," Violet added.

"Even call in false alarms and spill the paint cans and trample the evergreens — and steal our petition?" asked Benny.

And no one said anything, because no one knew the answer.

*   *   *

The Aldens spent the rest of the day painting the upstairs. They were working on the narrow hallway when Steve called up from below. "Have any of you seen Sparky's blanket?"

"You mean that old blanket he sleeps on?" Jessie called down.

"Yes. I'm doing some laundry — sheets and stuff — and I'd like to wash it," Steve answered.

"It's not in his basket?" Jessie asked.

"No," Steve said. "Oh, well, don't worry about it. I'm sure it'll turn up."

"Unless a burglar took it!" Benny said, and everyone laughed.

Not long afterward, the Aldens were done painting. "What a difference a little fresh paint makes," Violet said, looking around to admire their work.

"I just hope all this work will change the town council's mind," said Benny.

The children packed up their supplies and carried them downstairs. They were getting ready to go home when they heard a voice coming from the back of the fire-house.

"What happened here?" It was Steve, and he sounded upset.

The Aldens hurried to the back and found Steve by the back door. He was carefully examining the lock.

"What's wrong?" Jessie asked.

"The lock is broken," Steve said. "I was going out back to get some fresh air when I noticed it."

"How did that happen?" Violet asked.

"It looks as if somebody intentionally broke it," said Steve. "This is a strong lock. It couldn't have just broken by accident."

"You mean someone broke into the fire-house?" asked Benny. "I was only kidding about a burglar stealing the dog blanket."

"When do you think this happened?" Henry asked. "Last night?"

"It must have," said Steve. "I left this way yesterday after we had dinner, and the lock was fine then."

"But the front door is always open. Why

wouldn't someone just come in that way?" asked Violet.

"Well, if you want to make sure no one sees you, the back door would be better," Jessie pointed out.

"We keep the back door locked for just that reason," Steve said.

"So you're saying someone broke in, and nobody heard it?" asked Henry.

"There were a couple of calls last night, so for several hours the place was almost empty. And the calls were false alarms," Steve said.

"The person who broke in might have called in the false alarms. That way whoever it was could make sure no one would be around," Jessie pointed out.

"I think you're right," Steve said.

"That's terrible!" Violet said. "Why would someone do something so awful?"

"Is there anything missing?" Henry asked.

"Other than Sparky's blanket, I haven't noticed anything," Steve said. "There isn't

much here of value anyway — except the television, and it's so old that no one would steal it."

"That's it!" Jessie said all of a sudden. "Maybe the thief *was* after something old."

"The antique silver pieces!" Henry cried.

Steve and the Aldens hurried over to the shelves where the trophies and speaking trumpets were stored. The bottom shelf was bare!

CHAPTER 9

The Final Clue

At first Steve and the Aldens just stared at the empty shelf. "I can't believe we didn't notice this before," said Steve, at last.

"It's so dark back here in this corner that you wouldn't notice unless you came and stood right in front," said Jessie.

"The old copper hose nozzle is gone," said Violet.

"And that really tall speaking trumpet," added Henry.

"I'm going to go tell Mike and call the

police," Steve said, his voice angry. "It's getting late, and you kids should be getting home. After all, the rally's tomorrow, and you need to get a good night's sleep. I'll call you if the police discover any clues."

"Are you sure there's nothing we can do?" Jessie asked.

"Thanks, but I don't think so," Steve said.

That night after dinner, the Aldens gathered in the boxcar to talk about the burglary.

"I've been thinking. Do you suppose the burglary has anything to do with all the other stuff that's been going on?" asked Benny.

"I've been wondering that, too," said Henry.

"It certainly explains all the false alarms. Someone must have been trying to get the firefighters out of the firehouse so he or she could come in and steal the antiques," said Jessie.

"But what about the spilled paint and the

trampled evergreens?" asked Violet. "How could those be connected?"

The children all thought for a moment.

Suddenly Henry gasped. "I know! Maybe the person has been trying to sneak in here all week. He or she might have tried the garage door first. Remember we left our paint cans right in the doorway?"

"You think someone tried to sneak in at night, didn't see the cans in the dark, and accidently knocked them over?" Jessie said.

"Exactly," said Henry.

"But the paint couldn't have just spilled out," Violet pointed out. "Benny had put on the lids. Right?" She turned to her little brother.

Benny squirmed uncomfortably. "Well, um . . . I started to. But then there was that fire alarm, and Steve said we could come with him to watch and . . ."

"Benny," Jessie said, "are you saying you didn't put all the tops on securely?"

"I'm not really sure," Benny said uncertainly.

Jessie sighed. "Try to be more careful next time. Anyway, we've got a bigger problem now."

"I've been thinking about the evergreens," said Violet. "Those window boxes are in the side windows, and the ground was all scuffed up below them."

"That's right!" Henry cried. "The person wasn't after our evergreens — he was trying to get in through those windows. The window boxes just got in the way!"

"That still doesn't explain why Rebecca had our petition," Jessie noted.

"No, it doesn't," Henry agreed. "And speaking of Rebecca, remember how interested she was in the antiques? She kept looking at them whenever she was here — even today."

"And remember she made that detailed drawing of them, and then seemed embarrassed to talk about it," Violet added.

"She also said something about old things being valuable," Jessie remembered.

"I just thought of something else," Benny

said. "When we first came in to her studio, she was talking on the phone about making a lot of money."

"That's right," said Henry. "Maybe she was planning to steal the trophies and sell them."

"Henry, when you showed Ms. Lerner and Rebecca around, didn't you say Ms. Lerner was interested in the antiques, too?" Jessie asked.

"She was," Henry recalled. "In fact, she was the one who told Rebecca that they were valuable in the first place."

"I think there's someone else we're forgetting," said Violet. "Mr. Frederick."

"That's right," said Jessie. "He keeps showing up here, and it doesn't seem that he's telling the truth about writing a book on Greenfield's historic buildings. He doesn't know anything about our town's buildings. Maybe he was really after the antiques."

The children heard the cuckoo clock striking in the house and knew that it was getting late.

"Maybe tomorrow we'll find some more clues," Henry told the others as he led the way back to the house.

The Aldens were happy to wake up to a bright winter morning that really wasn't very cold. "This will be a perfect day for the rally," said Jessie.

After lunch, Grandfather drove them to the firehouse. Steve and Sparky greeted them inside.

"Any news about the burglary?" Henry asked.

"No, but the police are working on the case," Steve answered.

Grandfather and Mike helped the children hang their banner on the front of the building. As they were putting it up, Ms. Lerner appeared.

"I hear you've had a burglary," she said to Mike.

"Yes, I'm afraid so," he replied.

"If there'd been a proper display case — with a lock — maybe those pieces would still be here," she said angrily. Then she walked away to join the small crowd that was gathering.

"Did you hear that?" Jessie whispered to Henry.

"Yes," her brother answered. "Do you think Ms. Lerner would have taken the pieces herself, just to create one more strike against the firehouse?"

"Maybe," said Jessie.

As more and more people showed up for the rally, Henry passed the petition around. More and more signatures were added to the already full page.

"Look, there's Rebecca," said Violet.

A woman right next to Rebecca was speaking loudly. "I think it's just terrible they're planning to tear down this beautiful old building."

"I know. They'll probably put up something big and modern that will look just awful," said the man next to her.

Violet knew that Rebecca must have heard what they were saying. She saw Rebecca sigh heavily, but she couldn't tell if Rebecca was angry or sad.

Then Mike stood up on a chair and began speaking. "I want to thank you all for coming today. I especially want to thank James Alden's grandchildren, Henry, Jessie, Violet, and Benny, who came up with the idea for this rally. They did all the wonderful posters you've seen around town, as well as this banner."

A murmur went through the crowd, and someone shouted, "Great job, kids!"

Mike went on, "As you know, the town council is thinking of tearing down our firehouse and putting up a new one. I've worked here a long time, and I know this place has some problems. But it's also got a lot of history, and it belongs here."

"That's right!" someone called out.

Mike continued speaking. "The Aldens have been helping us fix up the building, and I think it looks pretty good. I invite all of you to go inside and take a look. I hope that with your help, we can convince the town council that this building should stay."

Mike went on to tell a little bit about the history of the firehouse, back to the days when the pumpers were pulled by horses. Then he asked everyone to please sign the petition. When he finished, everyone cheered.

"Nice speech," Grandfather said, patting Mike on the back. The Aldens watched as Ms. Lerner and Rebecca walked away. They did not look happy.

When the crowd of people had gone home, Steve came over to the Aldens. "The rally was a real success," he told them. "You all have been working so hard — how about taking a break this afternoon?"

"Sounds good to me," said Jessie.

"How does a game of basketball sound?" Steve suggested. "Benny and me against Violet, Jessie, and Henry."

"Can you play basketball in your wheelchair?" Benny asked.

"You bet," Steve answered. "I even have a special sports wheelchair that's more flexible. Come on!"

As Grandfather left to go home, the children followed Steve eagerly out to the basketball court in back of the firehouse. In no time, Steve and Benny were winning, 10 to 4.

Just as Benny was running to the basket to take another shot, Violet pointed over his shoulder. "Hey, what's that over there?" she called out.

Benny was so startled that he lost control of the ball. It bounced away and rolled onto the grass. "Violet!" Benny said angrily. "Are you trying to make us lose?"

"No, really," Violet said, running over to the side. She reached down below a bush and picked up a small blue notebook.

"That looks familiar," said Jessie. "Didn't we see someone carrying that recently?"

"Yes, but I can't remember who. . . ." said Henry.

"Maybe there's a name on the inside." Violet opened the cover. "Oh, my goodness. . . ." she said as she read what was on the first page.

"What is it?" asked Benny.

"I think it's a clue to the burglary," said Violet.

"What's in there?" Jessie asked.

Violet took a deep breath. "Listen to this," she said, and began to read aloud: "*Silver speaking trumpet, 1890; copper hose nozzle, 1900; looks valuable — call Lenny to arrange a deal.*"

"That must have been written by the burglar," said Henry.

"If only we could remember who we saw carrying that notebook," said Jessie.

"I remember!" Benny cried.

CHAPTER 10

To Catch a Thief

"Well, who was it?" Jessie demanded.

"It was Mr. Frederick! *He* had a notebook with that gold design on the front," said Benny. "He must be the thief!"

"Wait a minute," said Steve. "We can't just accuse someone unless we're sure. I'm going to call the police. They should see that notebook."

Steve called, and two police officers arrived a few minutes later. They looked at the notebook and immediately agreed with the children. "It certainly seems that the man who owns this book had something to do with the burglary," said one of the officers. "We need to ask him some questions."

"But if he *is* the thief, we don't want to scare him off," the other officer pointed out.

"I could call him and just say that we've found the notebook and that he should come pick it up," said Jessie.

"Good idea," said the first officer. "We'll handle things when he gets here."

Henry looked up Ralph Frederick's number in the phone book and Jessie called him.

"I've been looking all over for that notebook," Ralph said when she told him what they'd found. "I must have dropped it when I was out in back the other day. I'll be right over to pick it up. Oh, and please don't look inside. It's some . . . uh, notes for my book, and I'd like to keep them private."

The police officers parked their car around the corner so Ralph wouldn't see it when he arrived. Then they waited in Mike's office, while Steve and the Aldens stayed in the living room. Not long afterward, they saw an old station wagon pull up in front. Mr. Frederick got out, looking nervous.

"Here's your notebook," Jessie said when he'd entered the firehouse.

"Thanks," said Mr. Frederick, turning to leave. "Gotta run."

"Mind if we ask you some questions first?" asked one of the police officers, stepping out into the living room.

Just then there was the sound of a dog barking excitedly out in front.

"That sounds like Sparky," said Jessie, running outside to see what was the matter.

The others followed her. They found Sparky standing by Mr. Frederick's car, his paws up on the back door. The back window was open and Sparky was looking inside.

"What is it, boy?" Jessie called. When she and the others looked into the car, they saw why Sparky was so upset. An old blanket was spread out across the back seat of the car.

"That's Sparky's blanket!" said Benny. "He must have been able to smell it."

"No, no, that's just an old — " Mr. Frederick began.

But it was too late. Everyone had already spotted what he had been trying to hide under the blanket. Peeking out from beneath it were a couple of silver trophies.

"The missing antiques!" cried Violet.

"Just as we thought," said one of the police officers. "We've been looking for a pair of thieves who specialize in valuable antiques. Their names are Ralph and Lenny. And I think we've just found Ralph."

"You weren't writing a book about historic buildings, were you?" asked Jessie.

Ralph shook his head. He knew he'd been beaten.

"But why did you take Sparky's blanket?" Violet wanted to know.

"I needed something to hide the antiques when I sneaked them out of the building. It was handy, so I grabbed it," Ralph explained.

"Did you knock over the paint cans and trample the evergreens?" asked Benny.

"I didn't mean to. I was just trying to find a way to get inside," said Ralph. "I tried the garage, but in the dark, I didn't see those paint cans. I was afraid the sound of them clattering gave me away. And I had paint all over my shoes, so I had to go home and change. The next night, when I tried to come in through the side windows, those window boxes got in my way."

"And you called in the false alarms, too, didn't you?" asked Henry.

Ralph nodded.

As the police officers walked off with Ralph, Benny said, "We've solved another mystery."

"With a little help from Sparky," Violet added, rubbing the dog's head.

Just then, an alarm began ringing and several firefighters ran out to the trucks.

"What is it?" Steve called to Christine.

"Fire in an abandoned building down by the river," she called back.

"Can we go watch?" asked Benny.

"I'll take you in my car," said Steve. "But we'll stay far away from the fire and out of the way of the firefighters."

As Steve's car approached the burning building, the Aldens began to smell smoke. Large flames were coming from the windows of the two-story building. Several firefighters with hoses stood around the outside, shooting streams of water up at the building. A couple of firefighters were standing up on ladders, spraying water into the top of the building.

Two firefighters came running out of the building, their oxygen masks over their faces. "They must have gone in to make sure there wasn't anyone inside," Steve explained.

Slowly but surely, the Aldens could see that the flames were beginning to die down. At last the fire was out.

"Wow, that was amazing," Benny said as Steve drove them home. "Especially those two who went inside the building. That takes courage. I want to be a firefighter when I grow up."

"It's hard work," said Steve, "and it's dangerous. But it's one of the greatest jobs in the world."

The following morning, the Aldens were just finishing breakfast when the telephone rang and Jessie answered it.

"That was Mike," Jessie said when she hung up. "He asked if we could come down to the firehouse right away."

"Did he say why?" asked Henry.

"No," said Jessie. "He just said it was important."

When the Aldens arrived at the firehouse, they found Mike, Steve, Ms. Lerner, and Rebecca waiting for them. Rebecca was holding a large rolled-up piece of paper in her hands and had a mysterious look on her face.

"We thought you should be among the first to see our plans for the new firehouse," Ms. Lerner told the children.

"You mean you're still planning on tearing the old one down?" Jessie asked. She couldn't believe it. "Even after the rally?"

"Why don't you take a look," said Rebecca, unrolling her drawing of the proposed new firehouse.

"That looks just like the old firehouse," Henry said, "but bigger."

"Exactly," said Ms. Lerner. And for the first time, she smiled at the children. "Rebecca has come up with a way to repair the old building and add a wing on to the side. That way there will be more room."

"And I've designed the new wing to match the old building," said Rebecca, pointing to one side of the drawing.

"That's wonderful!" said Violet.

"I can't believe we thought you two might be trying to hurt the old firehouse," said Benny.

"Benny!" Jessie said, embarrassed.

"What do you mean?" asked Ms. Lerner.

It was too late. There was nothing the Aldens could do but explain.

"You always seemed so angry," Violet said to Ms. Lerner.

Ms. Lerner smiled again. "I was upset. I love old things, and it made me miserable to think that we'd have to tear this place down. But I knew the fire department had outgrown this building. The town couldn't afford two buildings. I couldn't think of any way around it. Until Rebecca's brilliant plan."

"We were afraid that maybe you'd even taken the antiques to convince the town council to tear down the firehouse," said Jessie.

"I would never do that! But it did upset me that those beautiful works couldn't be properly displayed. But now Rebecca has designed a special display area for them — with a lock," Ms. Lerner explained. "I can't believe you suspected me!"

"And you suspected me, too?" Rebecca asked in surprise.

"We thought you took our petition to try to stop us," Benny explained.

"*Took* it? You left it in my studio the day you stopped by!" she said.

"So that's what happened!" said Jessie. "Now I remember. We were showing it to you just before you took out your stack of drawings — "

"And I put them right on top of the petition," said Rebecca. "I found it later when I'd put the drawings away. You didn't think *I'd* taken the antiques, too, did you?"

The children nodded, slightly ashamed.

"But why?" Rebecca asked.

"You had been studying them so closely," said Violet. "We thought maybe it was because you were plotting to take them. You also said something about old things being valuable."

"I've always liked modern art, modern buildings. . . ." Rebecca began. She paused and looked down at her hands, then back up at the children. "Seeing those nozzles and speaking trumpets was the first time I really thought about the value of *old* things. And that's what led me to design a new wing on the firehouse, but keep the old part."

"Why were you studying the trophies so closely the day of the burglary?" asked Henry.

"Because I thought some were missing," Rebecca said. "But I wasn't quite sure, so I didn't say anything. I can't believe you thought I was a thief."

"We didn't really," said Jessie. "But we did overhear you say something on the phone about making a lot of money, and it made us wonder."

"Oh, that," Rebecca said, blushing. "I was talking to my husband, about this project. As I told you, I've only recently started out as an architect. This project is a big break for me. Mostly I'm excited about the work, but I have to admit, I'll also be happy to make a little money and pay some of my bills!"

At last all of the mysteries had been cleared up. "Thanks for all your help," Mike told the Aldens as they headed home.

"Anytime," said Benny. "Just give us a call next time you need a mystery solved!"

GERTRUDE CHANDLER WARNER discovered when she was teaching that many readers who like an exciting story could find no books that were both easy and fun to read. She decided to try to meet this need, and her first book, *The Boxcar Children*, quickly proved she had succeeded.

Miss Warner drew on her own experiences to write the mystery. As a child she spent hours watching trains go by on the tracks opposite her family home. She often dreamed about what it would be like to set up housekeeping in a caboose or freight car — the situation the Alden children find themselves in.

When Miss Warner received requests for more adventures involving Henry, Jessie, Violet, and Benny Alden, she began additional stories. In each, she chose a special setting and introduced unusual or eccentric characters who liked the unpredictable.

While the mystery element is central to each of Miss Warner's books, she never thought of them as strictly juvenile mysteries. She liked to stress the Aldens' independence and resourcefulness and their solid New England devotion to using up and making do. The Aldens go about most of their adventures with as little adult supervision as possible — something else that delights young readers.

Miss Warner lived in Putnam, Connecticut, until her death in 1979. During her lifetime, she received hundreds of letters from girls and boys telling her how much they liked her books.